From

The Author of A Questionable Hero

Book One in the Liston Pearce

Thriller Series &

Consumed By Fire

Book Two in the Liston Pearce

Thriller Series

Coming Out

A Novel

By

Stephen Gane

About The Author

I'm Stephen Gane and I was born in Bath, Somerset, in 1948. I left school with no qualifications. I then found employment as an apprentice chef. I joined P&O and worked on cruise liners for a while. Then I moved to London where I ended my cooking career as head chef of a London Club. My character Liston Pearce's love of cookery is something he shares with me. My second career was selling antiques which I did until I retired.

Suffering from dyslexia, I've always had problems with reading and spelling so writing a novel never entered my head. But, Christmas 2013, I had a dream and had to write the story. Seven weeks and three days later "A Questionable Hero" was finished. And now I have written the sequel and this novel about one of the characters.

I hope you enjoy reading my novels as much as I enjoy writing them.

My thanks to Angela Carter for
all the information
and advice she gave me while I
was writing this story.

Coming Out
by
Stephen Gane

Coming Out by Stephen Gane
© Stephen Gane 2015

Cover by fiverrcreator at fiverr

Editing by Edit-My-Book

Permanently Free on Amazon

A Questionable Hero UK

A Questionable Hero USA

Sign up for the author's New

Releases mailing list and get a free copy

of the second novel in the Liston Pearce

trilogy

"Consumed By Fire"

Click here to get started:

www.stephengane.com

CONTENTS

1. That's What I Want To Be When I Grow Up

2. Birthday Party

3. Don't Talk To Strangers

4. First Encounter

5. Brixton Riots

6. Shouldn't Have Said That

7. Bristol Or Manchester

8. Move To Bristol.

9. Awkward Meeting

10. A Visit To Mum.

11. Winston Tells All.

Chapter One

That's What I Want To Be When I Grow Up

It was Shrove Tuesday, 1971 Winston Oliver Sweet was eleven years old, just under five feet tall and a little on the plump side with a happy round face, short tightly curled hair and large eyes. He was wearing his school uniform of grey short trousers, blue blazer with the school badge sewn to the breast pocket, white shirt and the maroon and gold school tie.

He was sitting at his wooden school desk, which had seen a lot of love and abuse over the years. There were kick marks on the wooden legs. Idle and bored children had scribbled all over the inside and some kids had even tried to carve their names onto it. There was a little round hole at the top right hand corner, next to the groove along the top for holding your pens and pencils. Dark blue stains had seeped into the wood around the hole from the time when the desk used to have a small white china ink pot, which the ink monitor filled spilling nearly as much ink as he or she got into the pot. The inkwells had disappeared some time ago as children these days used fountain pens with cartridges and biros to write. The desk was shiny and well-polished from years of kids crooking their arms, trying to hide their answers from other children who were trying to copy their work.

Winston looked at the clock above the blackboard: ten minutes to go before the worst lesson of the day – PE. Winston hated PE. It was a double period as well, so that meant an hour in the gym with Mr Price, who used to play rugby for Wales. To take his mind off that awful prospect, Winston day-dreamed about getting home after school. His mum had said at breakfast that she would be making pancakes for tea.

Mr Evans, their form Teacher, was a short man, maybe five feet two inches tall, lean and wiry. His shiny bald head looked like it had been polished with a cloth. That was how he got his nickname of Bonehead. He was wearing a brown tweed jacket with leather patches covering the elbows, grey trousers and brown brogues. His chair squeaked on the wooden floor as he stood up and pushed it back with the back of his legs.

"Sweet, be a sweet thing and clean the blackboard before you go to your next lesson."

"Yes Mr Evans."Some of the kids sniggered as Bonehead tossed the blackboard rubber to Winston. Winston made a grab for it but missed and it fell by his feet with a clunk.

"Yes, Mr Evans."

Winston was the only black child in his class. There were seven other black boys in the school but they were all in other classes. They met up in the play-ground at break time and talk about girls and football, but Winston always seemed an outsider.

Winston picked the blackboard rubber up and walked to the front of the class. The rest of the class pushed and shoved their way out through the door.

"Quiet!! Or I will put you all on detention," Evans shouted.

Winston started to wipe the blackboard;

the white chalk dust drifted to the floor. Evans looked at him with disdain and thought, *He will never make anything of himself, not even get a job as a dust-man.*

Winston finished cleaning the board and placed the rubber on Mr Evan's desk.

"Run along, boy, or you will be late for your next lesson."

"Yes, sir."

Winston sauntered as slowly as he dared to the gymnasium. He pushed open the heavy double doors and walked in. The rest of the class were in different states of undress, in the process of changing into their navy blue shorts, black canvas daps and white vests.

"Come on, Sweet," Mr Price yelled.

"Sorry sir, I had to clean the blackboard."

This utterance was wasted on Mr Price.

Winston got changed as quickly as he could. He felt uncomfortable getting undressed in front of the other boys, and because he was late all the other boys had changed and were staring at him as he hopped on one leg, trying to get out of his grey short trousers and into his gym gear.

The gym was a nightmare as expected – climbing ropes, jumping over things, balancing on wooden benches – but worse was to come at the end, namely running round the gym like a maniac. Winston collapsed exhausted on a bench.

"Shower!" bellowed Mr Price

The showers consisted of a small tiled room at the end of the gym. Mr Price had turned the showers on a few minutes before. There were four showerheads for thirty seven boys so it was a bit of a squeeze. The slippery, soapy tiled floor was a death trap. Winston slowly undressed, wrapped his white towel around his waist and waited his turn to go into the shower, Billy Dyer stood behind him. Billy, the class bully, was a short stocky boy with a square face and a small button nose. He tried to pull Winston's towel away but Winston was holding on tight and Billy failed.

"I wonder if that brown will wash off the darky in the shower," Billy said to his mate, Martin in a loud voice.

"Quiet, Dyer," Mr Price shouted.

It was Winston's turn to go into the shower. He dropped his towel on a bench at the entrance to the shower where there were already seven or eight other boys shoving and pushing each other, laughing and joking around. Winston walked into the shower and it went quiet. He could hear the sound of water pounding on the tile floor and splashing off the other boys and onto him.

The boys parted to let Winston go under one of the showerheads. The warm water sprayed onto his short, tightly curled black hair, running over his shoulders and trickling down his body, and for a split second he forgot about where he was and enjoyed the warm water enveloping his body. Then he felt a push on his back. He instinctively put his hand up to save himself from being smashed into the tile wall but it was too late. The slippery floor took his feet and he landed in a heap in the shower tray. He looked up and saw Billy Dyer and the other boys hooting with delight.

Mr Price stormed into the shower room.

"Dyer, one hour's detention after school tomorrow. Forbes and Smith, you can join him."

"But sir, we didn't do anything. He slipped."

"I watched you push him, Dyer. Don't lie and make it worse for yourself, otherwise it will be a trip to the head master's office and you know what that means."

The boys grumbled.

"You OK, Sweet? Get up, dry yourself and get dressed."

"Yes sir."

Mr Price grabbed his arm and helped Winston to his feet.

"Dyer, make that two hours of detention."

"What for sir? I ain't done nothing else."

"My shirt is wet now, boy, and do not back-chat me."

Winston towelled himself dry and changed into his school uniform. It was the last lesson of the day so not long afterwards he walked down the school steps, past the tall grey stone buildings and out into a busy Brixton high street.

Winston had been born and brought up in Brixton, South London. His dad, Zachary Sweet, came to Britain from Jamaica in 1953, a few years after the first ship, *The Empire Windrush*, had arrived in 1948 with hopeful Caribbean men looking for work and to make a better life for themselves on the streets of London allegedly paved in gold.

Zachary Sweet was a bit of a wild child and part of the reason he left Jamaica was that he had gotten himself into some trouble back home. His parents shipped him off to the UK, hoping a cooler climate would cool his temperament. He was a snappy dresser and he usually wore a suit with wide trousers, shiny shoes and a white shirt

6

with a large multi-coloured neck tie, known as a kipper tie, which was tied in a big Windsor knot. His hair was short, slicked back with Brylcreem with a parting on the left hand side. He wore a hat, known as a pork-pie, made of light brown felt. It had a small brim with a darker brown silk band. He had sharp features with a protruding chin and was not as dark as a lot of Caribbean men.

Zachary was a handsome young man and soon got his girlfriend into trouble, so reluctantly they married in 1959. Winston was the outcome of the trouble. His mum, Lizzy, was just sixteen when she met Zach. He swept her off her feet and she soon became pregnant. Lizzy was a beauty: tall and slim with a great figure, long almost-black hair, high cheekbones, full lips and dark brown eyes. People who met her often thought she was Italian or Spanish and probably there was Mediterranean blood somewhere in her family.

Winston walked home, sometimes one foot in the gutter and one foot on the pavement up and down up and down. It had been raining earlier but it had stopped now. He dodged between big red London double-decker busses with his green duffel bag over his shoulder. He had a thirty-minute walk and he was thinking about the pancakes his mum was making for tea.

He was about five minutes from home and reached an alley with high red brick walls on both sides. He had walked a third of the way along it when a menacing, short, dark figure appeared at the far end of the alley. The figure stood feet spread well apart, his hands on his hips. Behind him was another taller figure. Winston tried to focus on them, and then he recognized them: it was Billy Dyer and Martin Simms. Winston hesitated, turned and started back down the alley but there was another boy blocking his exit. He turned with his back to the red brick wall, put the flat of one foot against it and waited. The three boys converged on him. His heart was pounding in his chest. He thought what would Billy the Kid would do in this situation: *shoot the three of them dead with his Colt 45*. Winston didn't have a Colt.

Then Billy Dyer was on him, his angry flushed face a few inches from his own.

"You fucking black piece of shit, you got me double detention," Dyer shouted.

"I didn't do anything, it was you who pushed me."

Billy's two mates were crowding Winston in on both sides. Winston was trying not to look at them, and gazed up between the two walls. He wished Batman or Superman would swoop down from the grey, darkening sky and rescue him, but this was not a comic book and he knew he was done for.

"Why don't you fuck off back to your own country?" Billy sneered.

"This is my country I was born here."

"My dad said all you blacks are comin over here and nickin all the jobs."

Winston felt a sharp blow to his stomach. He tried to defend himself as best he could but with three boys punching him his knees collapsed and he crumpled to the damp stone ground. Billy put the boot in and Winston almost passed out. Then, what seemed like a long way off, he heard someone shouting. Perhaps it was Superman after all. Moments later the three attackers had fled and a tall dark man stood over him.

"Are you OK, son? Can you get up?"

Winston looked up with tears running down his cheeks at the helmeted policeman standing over him.

"I think so."

The young policeman grabbed Winston under his arm and helped him to his feet. He bent over and looked Winston in the eyes.

"Do you know those boys? What did they want?"

"They're from my school, they think I told on them."

"Where do you live?"

"Not far, in one of those flats at the end of the alley."

"Come on let's get you home. What's your name?"

"Winston Sweet, officer."

"Will there be anyone at home?"

"Yeh, my mum. We're havin pancakes for tea."

"Do you like pancakes Winston?"

"Yeh, love um."

The policeman walked with Winston to the block of flats where he lived. They climbed the concrete steps and walked along a balcony with an iron railing running along one side that looked out out over a once-green, grassed area that was now brown mud with two dead trees and dog turds.

"Number thirty-three, officer, just here."

Winston pushed the faded green door open and walked in.

"Mum, mum, there's a policeman here."

Lizzy was washing up in the kitchen at the end of the corridor. She picked up a tea towel and dried her hands. She hurried to Winston.

"What's happened?"

"He got picked on by some bullies on the way home from school," the policeman said.

Lizzy looked at Winston and cupped his face in her hands.

"You have a bloody nose. What have they done to you, my love?" She turned to the policeman. "Did you catch them? Do you know who they are? Will you tell the school?" Lizzy asked the officer.

"No, they ran off when I shouted. I'll log it when I get back to the station, and my sergeant will tell me how to proceed."

"Do you want a cup of tea, officer?"

"Thank you, that would be nice."

Lizzy disappeared into the kitchen. The police officer pulled the tight leather chinstrap from under his chin, took his helmet off and sat on the settee with the helmet on his knee.

Winston noticed the silver badge on the front of the helmet. It said METROPOLITAN POLICE with a big ERII in the centre.

"How long you been a policeman?" Winston asked.

"About three years now."

"Have you ever killed anyone?"

"Noo, not yet! There is more to police work that that, Winston."

Lizzy brought the tea in and placed it on the small glass coffee table. The policeman talked some more about being with the police force; about how he felt he was doing something positive and good for the community. He finished his tea and looked at Winston.

"If you have any more trouble with those

boys, pop into the station and I will sort it out."

"Thank you, officer," Lizzy said.

She showed the policeman to the door and then turned back to Winston.

"You get in the bath and give me all your school uniform. I will have to get it clean for you to go to school tomorrow."

"Are we still having pancakes for tea?"

"I suppose so. Go get your bath, and wash behind your ears."

"Yes Mum."

Winston slipped his stiff bones into the warm bath. The water eased the aches and pains which were starting to make themselves felt after that beating. He was remembering the kind policeman. He thought, *I wouldn't mind being a police detective when I grow up, like on the TV – catching criminals and shooting people.*

Chapter Two

Birthday Party

It was Winston's thirteenth birthday. It was a Saturday, so no school. He woke early and, still in his blue and white striped pyjamas, he hopped out of bed, pulled his blue and grey slippers and pushed his bedroom door open. The Sweet family home was on the second floor of an old and rundown tenement on Coldharbour Lane, not far from the bustling and colourful Brixton market. They had lived there for two years Zachary had rented it after having to get out of their last place a bit quick. It was a two-bedroom flat with a kitchen and a sitting room at the back which had a large picture window looking out on to a small car park and the communal waste bins. Winston's bedroom door opened into the sitting room. The sun was just starting to rise through the lace curtains which covered the window. Winston walked across the brown-patterned carpet and opened the door into the kitchen. Mum and Dad were waiting and immediately started singing.

"Happy birthday to you,

"Happy birthday to you,

"Happy birthday dear Winston,

"Happy birthday to you."

Winston grabbed his mum and she bent down and kissed him on the cheek.

"Happy birthday son, lookin forward to yer party this afternoon?"

"Sure am, Dad. You gonna be here."

"I will try and get off work a bit early and

catch the end."

"You presents are on the kitchen table, son."

Winston's eyes flashed to the table. There were three parcels all wrapped in pretty coloured paper, and three cards.

"Can I open them now, Mum?"

"Don't you want to wait until your party this afternoon?"

"No way."

"Go on then."

Winston took the biggest parcel first. It was light. He shook it – it rattle. He carefully unwrapped it. It was Super Spirograph, a drawing toy. He opened the box to find was a set of plastic gears and other interlocking shape-segments, such as rings, triangles, or straight bars. All the edges had teeth to engage any other piece.

"Great, Mum! Thanks, Dad!"

Lizzy and Zach looked at each other with a warm smile.

Zach said, "I'd better get off or I won't be back in time for the party."

"Can't you wait until he has opened the other two presents?" begged Lizzy.

"Be quick then."

Winston unwrapped the second smaller parcel. It was an Action Man Talking Commander.

"Thanks Mum and Dad! It's just the one I want to go with my other Action Men."

The third present was a selection box of chocolate bars: Mars Bar, Milky Way and some others.

His dad come over and said, "Happy Birthday, Winston, I'll see you later."

"Bye Dad, thanks for the prezzies."

Zach picked up his jacket which was draped over a kitchen chair and walked out the door.

"Come on, open your cards," smiled his mum.

Winston opened the cards. There was one from Mum and Dad, one from Auntie Jean and Uncle Ted, and the third was from Lizzy's mum, Granny Mary.

"Come on, let's have some breakfast. Then we need to go shopping and get some cakes for your party."

"OK Mum."

Winston sat at the Formica-topped table and his mum prepared toast and jam and a cup of tea. Winston enjoyed his food and ate it all with gusto. After breakfast Winston and his mum got ready to go shopping. They locked the door and walked along the balcony. Someone had been sick there the night before. Lizzy and Winston skirted around it – the smell was vile.

"Bloody scum," Lizzy muttered under her breath.

It was a short walk to Brixton Market where they encountered the usual intoxicating mixture of colours and smells, with all races and creeds of people shoving and vying for the best place in the queue, the best deals. The smell of cooking wafting into the air from traders selling street food, the noise of traders shouting their wares and trying to persuade customers to part with their hard earned cash for something they didn't need.

There was also a slightly dangerous feel to the market too. There were pickpockets at work, and people trying to sell goods which were stolen or fake gear, but Winston felt the excitement. He felt alive. He watched everything that was going on.

He still hankered after being a policeman when he left school and so he pretended he was an undercover agent as he walked through the market with his mum. Lizzy bought vegetables and a new pink blouse. She went into the cake shop where she had ordered a birthday cake. The shop was near the end of the market. Winston had to wait outside while his mum collected the cake which was placed in a blue and yellow box and was tied with a blue ribbon. They walked home through the market back along Coldharbour Lane and into the tenement block. It was close on noon and Winston was hungry, which was not unusual.

"Do you want baked beans on toast?"

"Yes please, Mum."

"After you have had something to eat, I need to get on making sandwiches for you party so you play with your new games in the living room."

"I can help with the sandwiches if you want?"

"No, it's your birthday, but thanks anyway."

Winston and Lizzy ate their baked beans on toast and Winston was banished to the front room to play. He sat with his new Super Spirograph, trying to work out how to use it. His mind drifted. He only had five friends coming to his birthday party, but Terry Richardson asked if could bring a friend of his so there might be six.

The afternoon sailed into early evening.

His friends were coming at four thirty and hopefully his dad would be home just after that. Zachary Sweet worked as a porter at Smithfield Meat Market. It was normal for him to start work early in the morning and often he would be home by one in the afternoon, but today they had a special order which meant he couldn't finish until later. By the time he got back to Brixton it would be well after four.

"Go and wash up, your friends will be here soon," Lizzy shouted from the kitchen.

"OK Mum."

Winston packed his new toys away and went into the small bathroom. He washed his hands, pulled faces in the mirror, ruffled his hair with his hands and went into the kitchen.

"Take some of the sandwiches into the front room and put them on the table," said his mum.

He heard the key turn in the lock.

"It's Dad!" he smiled.

Zach walked into the sitting room.

"How's the birthday, boy?"

"Good, Dad, you OK?"

"Yep. I'll go and wash and help you set up ready for your friends."

Winston helped his mum set the table. There were salmon spread sandwiches, cucumber sandwiches, sandwich spread sandwiches, Mr Kipling cherry bakewells, Cadbury's chocolate mini-rolls wrapped in blue and gold foil paper, chocolate fingers, orangeade, Coca-Cola and lots of other teatime treats.

Just after four-thirty the first two boys knocked at the door: brothers Rob and Mike Turner. Mike was older than Rob and Winston by a year. They lived in the block opposite. Then Terry arrived with his friend. Winston had only known Terry a short time: they met one day in the park while they were both on the swings. Terry was a year older than Winston and lived in a better part of Brixton.

Terry introduced his friend. "This is my friend, Peter."

Winston looked at Peter. He was three or four inches taller than Winston, slim with blond wavy hair which curled just past his ears, soft white skin, a narrow face with big deep blue eyes and long eye lashes. He wore a white shirt which was open at the neck and this revealed his elegant neck. He had a pale blue hand-knitted tank top and light grey long trousers. Winston was star-struck; he thought Peter looked like an angel. Winston thrust out his wavering right hand. Peter took hold of Winston's hand, warm, soft as a silk scarf. Electricity passed between the two boys. Winston was unsure why he felt this way. He had never met anyone he'd had this instant bond with before.

Peter passed him a little box wrapped in pretty blue paper. Winston took the present.

"Thank you, Peter," he said with a quiver in his voice.

"Put it with the other presents. You can open them all when your other friends get here," Winston heard his mum say from behind him.

A few moments the last two boys arrived, Ron Hammett and Albert Bolton both Winston's mates from school. They each gave Winston a small present and he placed them on the sideboard with the others. He glance at Peter's small box and wondered what was inside it.

Zach had organised a few party games before tea. There was pass the parcel, which Ron won, and musical chairs. There were five chairs in a line. Zach stood with is back to the people in the room and placed the needle on the record. Gary Glitter started singing, 'I'm The Leader of the Gang'. The six boys started dancing around the chairs. Then Zach stopped the music and there was a scramble for the five chairs. Terry missed out. Hoots of laughter filled the room. Lizzy took one of the chairs away. Zach started the record. Round the boys went, all hovering around an empty seat. Mike was the next one to be out, then his brother, Rob. Now there were three boys and two chairs, and Albert was the next to go. One chair, and Winston and Peter left. Zach started the music up again. Round the boys went both holding the top of the chair and trying to stay as long as they could when it was their turn to face the seat. Lizzy and the other boys tried to egg them on. The music stopped. Both Winston and Peter dived for the seat. Winston just got there first and Peter sat on his lap. Winston could smell the slight body odour coming from Peter's perspiring body, and he breathed it in, not knowing why. Peter sat on Winston's lap and crooked an arm around his neck. Winston felt elated.

"I won!" Winston squealed.

"I let you," Peter answered in a warm, low voice.

Everyone laughed.

"Tea-time," Lizzy shouted from the kitchen.

Zach and the boys rearranged the chairs around the table and they all sat down.

"Who wants orangeade?" Lizzy said, unscrewing the top of a bottle with a fizz.

They all sang 'Happy Birthday' and then tucked into the birthday tea. After a while Zach and Lizzy disappeared into the kitchen Zach returned a few minutes later and turned the light off. Lizzy came into the room with a large birthday cake with thirteen candles and placed it in front of Winston. Peter noticed how the flickering from the candles illuminated Winston's face in a warm glow. Winston blew the candles out with one mighty blow.

"Make a wish, make a wish," everyone shouted.

Winston wished Peter would become his best friend but didn't tell. Winston cut the cake and Lizzy shared it out with everyone there.

"Open your presents, Winston," Zach suggested.

Winston opened the presents carefully: some marbles from Albert, sweets from Ron and Terry, and Rob gave him a set of metal puzzle rings. Winston left Peter's present until last; the anticipation was almost unbearable. He picked up the small box and carefully unwrapped it. Inside the blue wrapping paper was a dark blue cardboard box with a small golden cross on the top. He carefully opened it, uncovering a small piece of black foam rubber. Lizzy and Zach were peering over his shoulder wondering what was under the foam. Carefully Winston pinched the foam and lifted it, and there was a small round silver medallion. Impressed into the silver was a standing figure of a man with a beard holding a long staff in his hand. He was wading across a river carrying a small child on his back who had a halo around his head. Around the edge were the words 'St Christopher Protect Us'. Winston picked the medallion up. He felt the room go quiet: it was as though he had suddenly lost his hearing. He held it up by the tiny silver ring attached to the top of the medallion, then the room was filled with noise again.

"That's beautiful," smiled Lizzy. The she looked at Peter and asked, "Are you Catholic?"

"Yes, Mrs Sweet."

Winston seemed unable to speak for what seemed to him like ages but was only a second or two.

"Say 'thank you' to Peter, son," his dad told him politely.

"Thank you, Peter."

"I have a chain in my jewellery box that should be OK for that." And Lizzy disappeared into the bedroom. She soon returned with a long silver chain. Winston threaded the St Christopher onto the chain and Lizzy fastened the catch around Winston's neck. He tried to look at the St Christopher but the chain was too short so he sort of peered at it at a slant.

The party ended and all the boys said their goodbyes.

Winston was getting tired. He cleaned his teeth, washed his face and put his blue and white striped pyjamas on, then walked into the living room where his mum and dad were watching TV.

"Thanks, this has been the best birthday ever."

"Come here, son." Zach beckoned him over and gave him a hug. Winston kissed his mum and said, "Nite nite."

Winston went into his bedroom, kicked

his slippers off and climbed into bed. His mum had already placed a hot water bottle in his bed so he snuggled down. He went over the day in his mind and thought about Peter. He pinched the silver medallion around his neck and drifted off into a restful sleep.

Chapter Three

Don't Talk To Strangers

The next few weeks were difficult for Winston. He couldn't quite get Peter out of his mind. He cherished the St Christopher Peter had given him – it was the last thing

he touched at night before drifting off to sleep. He had a longing, a gnawing in the pit of his stomach, an ache which only thinking of Peter could seem to make better.

Peter went to the Catholic school over a mile away from Winston's. He was not sure where he lived, so he needed to find Terry and then find out where Peter played. Winston went to the park where he'd first met Terry. He went every evening after school until one evening Terry was there with Peter. Winston was overjoyed. He ran over to the two boys.

"How yha doing?" Winston asked, looking at Peter.

"All right, you?" Terry replied.

"OK, good party wasn't it."

"Sure was, I was stuffed. Your mum and dad are great," Terry remarked.

"What do you want to do?" Winston said.

"Don't know. Go and play on the swings?"

The three boys ran off towards the area with the swings and roundabout. They jumped on the swings and had a competition to see who could swing the highest. Terry won. Then they tried the roundabout to see who could stay on the longest without feeling sick. Terry won again.

"Anybody got any money?" asked Winston.

"I still have some pocket money left," Peter said

"If you lend me some I'll buy us some sweets."

"I'll get them."

The boys ran as fast as they could across the park to a gate. On the opposite corner there was a newspaper shop. The boys burst through the doors.

"Steady on, you lot," scolded the shopkeeper, a fat man with his shirt sleeves rolled up.

They bought some sweets to share. Peter paid and then they bounded back to the park to play a while longer before it was time to go home.

***

Weeks and months went by. It was the nearly the beginning of the summer holidays. Lizzy and Zach were taking Winston for a week by the seaside. They had rented a caravan near Southend-on-Sea. The family had been there before and they enjoyed the sea and sand, the shops and cafés.

The last day at school before the summer break was always a good day. The teachers and pupils were much more relaxed and they finished at lunch time so Winston was home early. He was still getting bullied and hustled at school, kids still called him names – 'jungle bunny' was the name of the moment – but he was able to take it all in his stride and it only affected him on the odd occasion.

Dad was working and Mum was shopping so he used his own latch key to get into the house. He made himself a jam sandwich and drank a glass of milk, got changed and then he was off to the park. He was sitting on the swings, waiting for his friends, when he saw a tall man walking towards him. He was late thirties or early forties with a bald patch, and wearing a mid-length navy mac.

"Hi son, got the time?" the man asked.

Winston's mum and dad had told him not to talk to strange men. He wasn't sure what to do but just then Terry came running towards the swings. He sat on the swing next to Winston.

"No sorry don't have a watch."

"What did he want?" Terry spluttered, a little out of breath, as the man started to walk away.

"Just wanted to know the time."

"He was probably a homo."

"What's a homo?"

"A dirty old man. They try and get boys to go into the bushes with them and pull their trousers down and play with their willies"

Winston started to blush.

Peter came walking along the path and sat on a swing the other side of Winston.

"What were you two talking about?" he asked.

"Homos," Terry said

"What about them?"

"How they try and grab you into the bushes."

"Oh."

The three boys chatted some more about homos, bushes and willies then they dismounted from the swings and walked up a small grass bank across a narrow road and around a path to the duck pond.

Terry picked up some flat stones and tried without much success to skim them across the pond.

"These stones are useless," he huffed.

"Or it could be you," Peter suggested.

"I'm good at skimming stones."

"Yeh looks like it."

They walked around the pond and the three sat on a cast-iron-framed park bench. It had wooden slats to sit on and after a while it felt like you had grooves in your bum. Winston was sitting next to Peter, and as he looked at him, his golden locks just curling around his ear, he had a sudden urge to stroke his hair. Without thinking he stretched his hand out and gently touched Peter's hair. Peter flinched and jerked his head away.

"What are you doing?" Peter spoke with an accusing look in his eyes.

"Um, you had some grass in your hair and I was just trying to flick it out."

"You sure you're not a homo?" Terry jibed with a grin the size of Chelsea bridge.

"Don't be so daft, course I ain't a homo."

They joked around a bit longer then the park keeper walked past so they decided to move on. At some time after four they made arrangements to meet the next day and all went their separate ways home.

Winston walked along the balcony to his flat door and let himself in.

"Hi Mum."

"Hi love, what you been up to?"

"Been to the park with the boys."

"Won't be long now until we go away."

"Can't wait."

"Your dad was on early shift this morning so he's sleeping. As soon as he wakes up we'll have tea."

"What we havin?"

"Fish fingers, chips and peas."

"We got a pud?"

"There's some rice pudding for afters."

"Great, I love rice pudding."

"Go and watch TV for a while but keep it down low."

"OK Mum."

Winston went into the sitting room and switched the TV on. He caught the end of Blue Peter, then he heard his dad get up.

"Go wash your hands." His mum shouted from the kitchen.

Winston went to the bathroom and washed. By the time he had gone back into the kitchen and turned the TV off, it was time for tea.

The family sat around the small table in the kitchen. It was a light and airy place with a small window looking out onto the back. The sink was in front of the window and on the small window shelf there was a pot of African violets. The gas cooker was quite old but Lizzy kept it well maintained. There were a couple of wall units around the walls and a long worktop.

Winston started to tuck into his fish fingers.

"What are homos, Dad?"

Zach's fork with half a fish finger stuck on the prongs stopped mid-way between his plate and his mouth. Lizzy looked at Winston in horror.

"Where did you hear that word?" Zach

said replacing his fork on his plate. Both parents stared at the boy.

"Terry used it in the park."

"Why did he say it?"

"Because this bloke started talking to me."

"What did he say?"

"He asked if I had the time."

"Was that all? Did he touch you?"

"No, he just asked me if I knew the time."

Winston could feel the tension in his parents' voices. His mother was breathing hard.

"Are you sure that was all that happened?"

"Yes Mum, honest."

He could feel his parents relax a little.

"So who told you about," a slight pause "homos?"

"Terry, he said they are dirty old men."

"Was that all he told you?"

"Yes that was all. So what is a homo?"

Zach took a deep breath "Well, son, homo is short for homosexual. They are men who like other men."

"What's wrong with that, Dad? You like your friends, don't you?"

"Yes, but it's different with homosexuals."

"Why Dad?"

"It just is, Winston, believe me."

Winston could feel his dad's discomfort. He knew he was having trouble explaining what homosexuals were so he backed off with his questions, but he was curious and was determined to find out, just not at this moment.

"You will understand when you're a bit older," his mum whispered, resting her hand on his arm and squeezing it.

"OK."

27

"Just make sure you don't speak to any strange men, and if anyone talks to you who you don't know run away and tell a policeman."

"I want to be a policeman when I leave school."

"We know, Winston, you keep telling us!"

They returned to their fish fingers, which were getting cold.

"Shall I warm our tea up in the oven, Zach?"

"No love, it'll be fine."

After they finished tea Zach helped Lizzy with the dishes. Winston was in the living room watching TV, and he could hear his parents whispering in the kitchen. He knew it was about the conversation they'd had over tea.

After they finished washing up, Lizzy and Zach watched TV with Winston until it was his bedtime. Winston kissed his mum and dad goodnight and went to bed.

He lay there for some while with his bedside light on, wondering about the day. He was confused about homos, about why Peter pulled away from him in the park, about being a policeman... thoughts, thoughts.

Chapter Four

First Encounter

It was 1976 and Winston was now sixteen years old. His dad had sat him down in the living room a year or so earlier and tried to tell him the facts of life, about the birds and bees. Winston was not sure who was the most embarrassed out of him or his dad. He had learned about sex, homosexuality, dirty old men, VD and the like from his friends and classmates at school. He was still good friends with Peter and Terry. They still met after school but not so much at the park now. They met often at a coffee bar in Brixton called the Latin Quarter it still served frothy coffee in glass cups with glass saucers. They listened to the latest records on the juke box and Terry talked about girls and how far he had got with them.

Winston and Peter weren't quite as interested in girls as the rest of their mates. Winston like girls and didn't have a problem with them. He actually had quite a lot in common: they seemed to like the same music and he was interested in fashion. But when it came to going on a date with a girl, which he did on a number of occasions, and it came to kissing it felt strange and alien to him. One time a girl had put her tongue in his mouth. He was shocked. He joined in but he never wanted to do it again.

He like to listen to pop music, and Elton John and the Jackson Five were two of his favourites. The word 'gay' was beginning to be bandied around. It didn't sound so threatening and crude as 'homo' but the meaning was the same. At night in bed, when his hand found his penis it was Peter and other good-looking male movie and pop stars he fantasized about. Winston tried to suppress these feelings. He was in denial. He tried to pretend he was not gay but the thought kept creeping into his head. He could control it during the day, but when he was on his own at night the feelings just overwhelmed him. He had feelings of guilt, but why, he did not know. What would his parents say? He had to pretend there was no other way. If, as he hoped, he could join the police force and become a detective then how would being homosexual impact on this decision?

***

He had not long finished his exams at school and when the results came through there were better than even he expected. His dad wanted him to stay on at school and maybe go to university. Winston and his mum visited the careers officer, bit Winston only had one thought: what was the best way to join the police.

The careers officer told him he could apply to become a police officer when he was eighteen years old, but before that he could apply to be a volunteer police cadet now and it might help him later when he was older. Winston was slightly disappointed, but if that was what he had to do then so be it. Being a volunteer police cadet meant going to weekly meetings to learn about different aspects of police work, the law, how to deal with the public, crowd control and so on, and at weekends they put some of this into practice stewarding rallies and doing general duties.

Nothing too complicated or difficult, but it gave a brief taste of police work.

Winston sent in his application papers in and after a short while he was accepted into the organization. Winston had another decision to make: he had his part-time police volunteer cadet duties but was he to stay on at school or get a job until he turned eighteen? He talked to the police officer who was in charge of the cadets. He was an old-school copper coming up to retirement age. He was a large man with a round red nose. *Probably from drinking too much,* Winston thought. His name was Stan but they had to call him sergeant or sir. He explained that, as he saw it, police-work had little to do with school qualifications. As long as you had intelligence, could read, write and add up then that was the most all you needed to become a good policeman. Later in his career Winston discovered this was not the case.

Winston decided to get a job and earn money. He could save some of his wages, give some to his mum to help with the housekeeping and spend the rest on himself. He visited the job centre a few times and eventually he was interviewed for a job as a trainee manager at Tesco's supermarket. 'Trainee manager' was a bit of a misnomer as he was just a general helper, cleaner, shelf-stacker and gopher. He started at eight in the morning, had an hour for lunch and finished at four-thirty in the afternoon.

Winston had worked there for about six months and had been accepted by his work mates. They took the Mickey out of him but it was all good-tempered and light-hearted. A new part-time worker started as a shelf packer in the evenings. He was older than Winston, about eighteen. He did weight training and circuit training at a nearby gym. There was a cross-over time when they had to stack shelves together and they hit it off straight away.

His name was Roger. Like Winston he was a mixed-race child with a black father and a white mother. One evening Winston arranged to meet Rog after he finished his shift shelf packing. They were both keen on checking out a boxing club that had been opened in Brixton. Winston thought the boxing would help him with his police career and Rog just wanted to get even fitter than he already was.

They found the place easily. It was down a sidestreet off one of the main streets in Brixton.

Jim Duggan's Boxing Club was on the lower ground floor of what looked like an old factory building. They walked down a flight of concrete steps and past faded and peeling cream-painted walls. At the bottom there were two solid wooden swing doors with small painted-out glass windows.

Rog pushed the doors open. They had a stiff spring holding them and it was a bit of an effort to open them.

"Bloody hell, you need to be a strong man even to get into the place."

"Lightweight," Winston smirked.

The two young men walked into a large room. There was a boxing ring in the centre, about four feet off the ground. Around the sides there were punch bags hanging from the ceiling on chains. In one corner there were two speedballs: leather punch-balls hanging from the ceiling on a small arm which, when you hit them, bounced and then you hit it again. One young guy was on one of the speedballs, hitting it right then left in a mesmerizing beat. Two men were in the boxing ring one with boxing gloves and wearing a red face mask, the other with hand pads, they were sparing. There was an old guy shouting at the man with the gloves.

"Jab, jab, left hook, feint, hook, for God's sake move your feet, stop! Stop! Go get showered."

The old man turned and looked at Rog and Winston. He was about five feet seven inches tall, in his late fifties, skinny, but you could tell he was still strong. His blue-grey eyes were full of determination and drive. He had on a pair of baggy track suit bottoms, old sweaty-looking trainers with no socks and a T-shirt which was once probably white but now looked a dirty grey.

"Hi boys, how can I help?"

He walked over to Rog and looked him up and down.

"You look fit, boy, do you work out much?"

"A bit. We want to learn how to box."

The old man looked at them and let out a laugh.

"You should have come to me ten years ago boy."

He looked at Winston.

"Don't think there is much I can do for you, son. Maybe get you a lot fitter, but a boxer, no chance."

Rog said. "Can we give it a go for a few weeks?"

"Sure, give it a trial for a month. Then if you prove me wrong and you've got a bit of spirit, sign up."

"Great, where do we start?"

"George," the old man shouted and a big black guy ambled over.

"Yes boss."

"Go through a warm up with these two, then push ups and some light weights. Then, if they are still standing, let me have them back."

"Yes boss."

For the next three quarters of an hour they never stopped. George talked them through the warm up, then push ups, sit ups, body curls, then some weights. He then gave them a bottle of water and took them back to the boss.

The boss looked at them Rog didn't seem too bad but Winston was so tired he could just about stand.

"Shower boys, then back tomorrow."

Adam showed them to the shower room and left the two of them on their own.

"That was hard work," Winston gasped as he slumped on the wooden slatted bench trying to unlace his trainers.

"You should stop smoking – that would help, man. He's a fuckin slave driver," Rog said.

The two young men stripped off and walked into the warm shower. Rog was standing with his back to Winston. He looked at his well-defined muscles, his chocolate brown skin, his strong supple body, the warm water cascading down his body mixed with soap lather from washing his hair and body. Winston was getting aroused; he could feel a strengthening in his penis. Rog turned around and looked at him and noticed straight away that Winston was aroused. He went over to Winston and, with the warm water cascading down their bodies, Roger kissed

Winston on the lips. Winston's heart was racing. He stopped breathing for what seemed like a long time. Winston kissed Roger back and they held each other. Rogers hand traced Winston's body and he gently cupped his balls in his hand.

"We can't do much here, let's go back to my place," Roger whispered into Winston's ear, his warm breath making Winston even more eager.

They dressed and went to Roger's flat, a studio bed-sitter above a betting shop. The next few hours were Winston's first serious sexual encounter. They made love until they were exhausted.

The affair lasted another two and a half months then Roger told Winston he had been offered a place at Manchester University doing a teaching course. Winston was heart-broken. They kept in touch for a while, writing, the odd telephone conversation, then the love affair gently fizzled out. Winston carried on with the training for a while but after Roger had disappeared from his life the boxing faded as well.

Chapter Five

Brixton Riots

It was the beginning of April 1981. The tenth to be exact. Winston was now twenty-one years old. He had finished his two-year probation to become, as he had always wanted since a child, a policeman. He looked the part in his Metropolitan Police uniform with his bobby's helmet perched on top of his round face. He had lost his youthful looks now and a few lines had started to creep across his forehead.

It was mild for April as he set off to the police station. He still lived with his mum and dad but he was thinking of getting a flat of his own. He'd had two more brief sexual experiences since his affair with Roger, but he was finding it hard to come to terms with his homosexuality so he immersed himself in his job and the police force. His dad was giving him trouble, saying he should get a girlfriend and start thinking about settling down. Winston had come to terms he was gay in his heart but it was a secret life he led and he didn't feel he could tell anyone.

Work started as usual. He walked his beat through the streets of Brixton with little to occupy his attention apart from people asking him the way to this place and that, and shouting at kids riding their bikes on the pavement. There was a quietness in the air. Lunchtime came and went and it was getting near the end of his shift. He headed back to Brixton Police Station to log off duty. The desk sergeant told him there was trouble brewing and all policemen had to be on stand-by in the area. So he sat and waited in the canteen for orders. He chatted to the other officers and they speculated on what was happening.

The call came about seven-thirty in the evening.

His squad were briefed at Brixton Police Station by a police inspector. They were told there was serious trouble on the streets of Brixton. They heard how the riot had started and how it was to be controlled, or at least how the inspector thought it was going to be controlled, but the outcome was a lot different.

All the officers were bundled into the back of black police Ford Transit vans and trundled off to Railton Road, the area where the rioting was taking place. As they exited the rear of the van, Winston could hear the shouting and noise from the area to his left. There were seven or eight police vehicles parked alongside the one he had just disembarked from.

"Whats going on?" Winston asked one of the officers.

"It's your lot. They've gone crazy, looting and causing mayhem."

"What do you mean, my lot?"

The officer turned away.

The next few hours were the worst in Winston's life. The Brixton Riots, as they were to become known, were in full flight.

"What the fuck in going on?" he heard one of the officers say.

"All the coons are going crazy."

"Well, we'll sort the black bastards out," another officer replied.

This was the last thing Winston wanted to

hear. He was disconcerted at some of his fellow officers. Most were there to control the crowd and do their job, but some were there for the fight and to cause trouble.

They were lined up at the back of the police vans waiting for instructions. A large plank of wood came flying from the crowd. It flew over the van, hit the roof with a bang and slid into the back of one of his fellow officers. The officers tried to help the injured man but they were getting in each other's way. An ambulance man arrived, and with the help of two other officers they supported him and took him away. This was the first of many injuries Winston would see before the night was out. Big bricks, blocks of wood and metal bars started raining down, bouncing off the police vehicles. Another policeman was hit by a bottle. The line of men he was in was told to retreat to a safer distance.

He was given a flimsy plastic shield and told to hold the crowd back. He and his colleagues were guided to the front of the police vans, where they were confronted by the enraged crowd, shouting, swearing and brandishing' anything they could lay their hands on. There were about seventy or eighty policemen in a row trying to wrestle the crowd back. His was the only dark-skinned face in the line-up. As soon as the rioters saw him he was singled out for abuse.

"Rasclat tratior."

"Fuckin pig."

"Bloodclot shit."

And all manner of other abusive and threatening behaviour was directed at Winston Sweet.

The sergeant in charge of the cordon saw

this and shouted, "Get that black man out of the line, he's causing more trouble than he is worth."

Winston fought his way back to the relative safety of the police vans. His thoughts were mixed up: in one way he was glad to be out of harm's way, but on the other hand he was upset being cursed by the black community and then being shouted at and abused by the police force he had always wanted to be a part of.

He decided at that pivotal point in his life to try and change the attitude of fellow officers as much as he could. He leaned against a police van with thoughts of despair and confusion racing through his mind.

More missiles were raining down now. Bottles crashed around him, stones flew past his head and bounced on the road.

"The bastards have broken through," he heard a policeman shout. Police officers were streaming past him now in full retreat and in disarray. Winston joined the push to get away. He turned around and saw that the mob of people were now smashing the police vans with iron bars and rocking them from side to side. Then there was fire – one of the vans had been set ablaze. All the action around the vans gave the police officer in charge time to regroup his men. He ordered a baton charge. All the police officers who still had their truncheons drew them; the ones who had lost theirs didn't have time to do much else but pick up some of the missiles the rioters had thrown.

"Charge!!!"

The police surged forward. The crowd in front of them had now set two vans on fire. They taunted the officers. The charge wasn't much of a charge, more of a creep, what with the crowd yelling and throwing things and the heat from the now blazing police van. The line of policemen inched forward.

The burning police vehicles were now a hindrance to the rioters and they retreated back to the safety of the larger crowd. This toing and froing went on for the next few hours. Winston saw many of his fellow officers and many rioters hurt. Blood flowed, injuries abounded, flames licked against the night sky, buildings were set alight. There were people with makeshift bandages holding faces and limbs. The fire brigade was prevented from putting out the torched buildings, looting was rife. It was a war zone.

The Brixton Riots went on all that night and all the next day. By the time the riot fizzled out, over one hundred police cars had been destroyed. There had been widespread looting and arson and hundreds of people had been injured. Winston made a vow to himself: he knew he could not change attitudes to black people by talk alone so he decided to be the best person he could – to be the best police officer he could and try and lead by example.

He returned home with a heavy heart. He was exhausted and bewildered by the events he had witnessed but he tried to see a positive side. It had changed his view of some elements of the police force and given him a purpose to strive for.

A few days later, the Home Secretary William Whitelaw commissioned Lord Scarman to head an enquiry into the riots, with the power to make recommendations. The findings were that the riots were a spontaneous outburst, due to a complex political, social and economic situation.

The report highlighted problems of racial disadvantage and inner city decline.

Scarman found unquestionable evidence of the disproportionate and indiscriminate use of 'stop and search' powers by the police against coloured people. Scarman recommended changes in training and law enforcement, and the recruitment of more ethnic minorities into the police force.

Winston read the report in full. He was sad that it had come to this, but hopefully good would come from it and peace and friendship would reign over the streets of Brixton.

Chapter Six

Shouldn't Have Said That

Police constable Winston Sweet worked hard. He performed well and did his duties better than most. He made a few friends on the force, but was still not accepted by some of his colleagues. He had been on numerous courses and was always in the top two or three of his class. His supervisor had noticed his potential for a while, but at first he tried to look the other way and not recognise how well Sweet was doing. But in the end he had to as he was outshining all the other PCs in his squad.

One day his supervisor called him into his office.

"Sit down, Sweet."

"Yes sir."

The man in charge of PC Sweet was a short man with a broad Scottish accent. His name was Sergeant John Stewart. He had been on the force for years, just hanging on and keeping his head below the parapet waiting for retirement.

"I've been keeping an eye on you, Sweet."

Winston felt a knot in his stomach.

"You are doing well, my boy. Do you see yourself as a long-term career policeman?"

"Yes sir, I have always wanted to be a copper."

"Good, good." Stewart began looking at a file in a green folder.

"I see from your last course you said you would like to become a detective?"

"Yes sir, it's what I've dreamed of."

"Dreamed of, ah. Well Sweet, there is a long way to go but I am recommending you to go on some extra courses to see how you shape up."

"What, detective courses?"

John Stewart looked at PC Sweet and frowned, which made his bushy eyebrows seem even thicker. Sweet then looked at Stewart a little harder: he not only had bushy eyebrows but he also had hair growing from his ears and poking out of his nose. PC Sweet tried not to stare but once he had noticed it, it was hard not to look.

"Is something wrong, Sweet? You look distracted."

"No sir, I'm just taken aback at the thought of maybe becoming a detective."

"OK, I'll set the wheels in motion. That's it, Sweet, you can go."

Winston stood up and saluted, turned and walked out. He walked along the corridor a little way then stopped rested his back against the wall, put his foot on the wall and looked at the ceiling. He took an enormous breath. A smile crept across his face and he was elated. One of the other PCs walked past.

"You OK, Winnie?"

Winston had acquired a nickname since he had become one of the boys. He didn't like being called Winnie but it was better than 'that black bastard', which he had heard often.

"Yeh, good. Stewart has told me he going to put me up for detective."

"Well done, mate, drinks on you later in the bar?"

"Sure."

Winston's mate walked down the corridor. *I could do with a ciggie,* Winston thought.

After his shift he met some of his colleagues at the pub across the road from the police station. He walked in The Duke of Wellington. The place was crowded, smoke-filled, grubby and smelled of beer. It was used mainly by off-duty police so there were plenty of familiar faces. He pushed his way to the bar.

"Hi Winnie," the barman nodded. "What you havin?"

The barman was West Indian. He had a skinny face like a skull with skin. His jet black dreadlocks perched on his head like a mop.

"A pint and a small whiskey."

The barman returned a few moments and placed his drinks on the beer-soaked bar towel.

"Eleven pounds twenty-six."

"Fuck, how much?"

"Everyone said you were celebrating and were in the chair. Make it eleven-fifty and I'll have one with you, Winnie."

Winston paid up and a big cheer rumbled around the bar. The barman walked back to Winston holding a small glass. He chinked it on Winston's beer glass and downed it in one swallow.

"Wow, I needed that. What ya celebratin Winnie?"

"My boss has put me up for detective."

"Great mate, we need more black folk on the force dooin good."

Winston stayed a while longer but he was eager to get home and tell his mum and dad.

A few weeks passed and nothing happened. He wondered if it had all been some sort of joke when he was called into Stewart's office. Winston knocked on the frosted window of his sergeant's half-glazed door.

"Come in."

"Sit down, PC Sweet. Your first course for the DC training will be next week. It's just a day course so no overnight stay."

"Thank you sir. What's it about?"

"It's just the introduction. They'll give you all the details on the course."

"How long will all the courses and training take, sir?"

"Six months or a bit longer."

"Then what?"

"You will have a personal development review, then wait for an opening somewhere."

"So I won't be able to stay in Brixton?"

"Unlikely Sweet, unless you are fortunate enough that someone is leaving or is promoted. Is that all?"

"Yes sir, thank you."

Over the next few months Winston went on a number of courses covering all aspects of detective work. On one occasion he had to stay overnight at a small guest house called The Glades, a 1930s period house with some fine Art-Deco features still in place. The two-day course he was attending dealt with procedural matters and the second day was to cover interviewing techniques.

He had finished the first day's training, which went well. He had returned to the guest house at just after six. He'd only had a ham roll for his lunch and a cup of tea so he was starving.

Dinner at The Glades was at seven-thirty so he went to his room, washed the grime of the day off his hands and face and sat in the lime green Lloyd Loom chair by the side of his single bed. He lit a cigarette and placed it in the ashtray on the small wicker table next to him. Winston picked up the notes he'd made during the day's course and started reading. His mind started to wander and he found he had to read the same piece over again.

"This is a waste of time," he said out loud.

He decided to go down into the lounge and see if he could have a drink, Winston stubbed the cigarette out into the small glass ashtray, put his jacket and went downstairs. He found the lounge on the left at the bottom of the stairs. He had to pass under a wooden arch into the oak-panelled room. It was decorated with geometric-patterned black and silver wallpaper and bold Art-Deco furniture graced the wooden-block parquet floor. There was a small bar in one corner of the room and on the counter was a small silver bell. He looked around; there was no one to be seen. He picked the bell up and looked at it. It was decorated with vine leaves and bunches of grapes. He thought, *If this was in Brixton it would have been nicked if it wasn't on a chain.* He tinkled the bell. Almost immediately a tall slim woman in her early twenties walked under the arch into the lounge.

"Good evening sir, can I get you something?" she offered, eying him up and down.

"Good evening, can I have a beer?"

"We only have bottled, sir."

"Bottled is fine. Do you have Guinness?"

The young woman picked up a bottle of Guinness from the shelf behind the bar and poured it.

"Do you want me to put it on your bill?"

"Oh, yes please."

46

"Room number sir?"

Winston pulled the key from is pocket.

"Number five."

The woman scribbled a note on a pad by the side of the till.

"You staying long, sir."

"Just one night. Please call me Winston."

"Yes sir, I mean Winston."

"Are you in for dinner?"

"Yes."

The two chatted some more. It turned out the young woman was the daughter of the owner and she and her mum and dad ran the place, with the help of a cleaner who worked mornings.

"My name is Samantha, but you can call me Sam."

Sam was about five feet seven inches tall. Her long, wavy, mousy hair fell around her shoulders. She was wearing a plum-coloured hand-knitted woollen cardigan over a white blouse and a pale blue pleated skirt. They chatted some more and Winston had the distinct impression she seemed quite interested in him. This made him feel a little uncomfortable.

"Would you like another drink, Winston?"

"I'll have a small whiskey. Can I buy you a drink, Sam?"

"Um, I'll have a glass of white wine."

The two talked for a while longer and then a man in his fifties strutted into the bar.

"Samantha, your mother needs some help in the kitchen I'll take over in here."

"OK Dad. Maybe see you later, Winston?"

"Sure."

Sam's father was ex-military, a drum-major in the guards. He was wearing highly polished brown shoes, cavalry twill trousers, a white shirt with a blue silk cravat tied around his neck and a dark blue blazer with three brass buttons. He had a round, shiny clean shaven face, thin silver hair and a small moustache.

"Good evening Mr Sweet, settled in your room OK?"

"Yes, it's fine."

"Are you at the police training at the Old Manor?"

"Yes, how did you know?"

"We get a lot of the trainees stay here, it's good business for us. How is it going?"

"It's going well. There's a lot to learn but I'm enjoying it. The instructor's a bit strict."

"That's what's missing from the youth of today: discipline. Two years' national service would sort all these yobs out. I suppose you see a lot in your job?"

"We get our share, that's for sure."

The dinner gong sounded in the hall: *bong, bong, bong.*

"That will be the lady of the house. Are you dining tonight, Mr Sweet?"

"Yes, I'm starving."

After dinner Winston returned to the bar for a nightcap. Sam was serving.

"Yes Winston, what can I get you?"

"I think I have a scotch on the rocks. You going to have one with me?"

"That's kind of you, I will."

Sam poured their drinks and Winston sat on a bar stool.

"Did you enjoy your dinner, Winston?"

"It was lovely."

"My mother is a good cook."

"She sure is."

"I must buy you a drink now, Winston."

"Thanks, you're going to get me drunk and I need to be fresh for the course tomorrow!"

"Another isn't going to hurt."

They sat and drank another, then another. It was soon gone eleven and Winston was the only one in the bar.

Sam said, "I need to close the bar now ."

"No problem, I must get off to bed anyway. I have a hard day tomorrow."

Sam walked through the small entrance to the bar. She stumbled a little and Winston caught her arm.

"Careful Sam, looks like you've had one too many."

Sam sidled up to Winston and looked at him. Her brown eyes met his and she tried to move her mouth closer to his. Winston pulled away a little.

"Don't you want to give me a goodnight kiss, Winston?"

"I don't think that's a good idea."

"Why not? It's only a friendly peck."

She was resting her body on his now with her hands on his shoulders. She tried to pull him forward to kiss him, but he turned his head away.

"What's wrong? Don't you like me?"

"It's not that, I'm gay."

Sam looked at him, aghast. Her eyes became narrow. She pushed his shoulders with the palms of her hand.

"You're a queer? A bum bandit?"

Sam turned and ran through the wooden archway into the hall, then Winston heard her run up the stairs. His heart was pounding. Was she going to call her father? Was he in trouble? He waited for a while: it was quiet. He walked into the hall and up the stairs to his room. He unlocked the door, still listening to see if there was any activity. He switched the light on and closed the door behind him. He leaned with his back against the door, still waiting and listening.

"Fuck!"

He went into the small en-suite shower room and half-filled the sink with cold water. He cupped his hands and splashed water in his face. His mind and body were still on edge with anticipation. He urinated, still trying to detect any noise apart from his water splashing into the toilet.

He went into the bedroom and sat on the edge of the bed.

"What the fuck did you say that for?"

Resting his elbows on his knees, he placed his heavy head in his hands, then sat up and brushed his hands over his hair. Cradling his head in his laced fingers, he looked at the light fitting hanging from the ceiling. There was no movement he could hear. All was quiet. He stood up and prepared himself for bed. He lay back on the pillow with just the small bedside lamp illuminating the room.

Why did I say I was gay? She is the first stranger I have ever come out and told I am gay. Am I stupid? I suppose I must come out someday, so perhaps it's a good thing, I wonder what will happen tomorrow?

Winston had a disturbed night's sleep, tossing and turning. The morning came and he packed his small rucksack and went down to breakfast. Sam was nowhere to be seen. He ate a good breakfast, glancing around the dining room looking for any sign of Sam. He paid his bill and collected the receipt, went back to his room, picked up his belongings and left.

Chapter Seven

Bristol or Manchester

It was now 1982. Winston was twenty-two years-old. PC Winston Sweet went on all the courses, did all the training and did his personal development review. He passed all the tests and reviews. Now came the agonizing wait for the final results.

His job on the force had settled into a routine of shift-work with general duties, walking his beat doing what he could to build community spirit between the black residents and the police. He helped out at a local youth centre in his spare time and tried his best to get the black kids he worked with to get involved in worthwhile activities.

A few more weeks passed by. Then one morning he was called into Sergeant Stewart's office.

"Come in and sit down, DC Winston Sweet," Stewart said with a smile.

"I passed, sir?"

"With flying colours! You were the top-rated candidate, passed in all categories. Congratulations, Sweet." Stewart stood up and offered his hand to DC Sweet. Winston shook his hand with delight.

"Well done, I knew you would do it. You've done me proud."

"Thanks you, sir."

"You can let go of my hand now, DC Sweet."

"Oh, sorry sir. What happens now?"

"You will get an official letter, and then you need to find an opening."

"So, I can't stay here?"

"No there are no vacancies for a DC here."

"How long will it take to find a post, sir?"

"Weeks, months... it depends where you apply and if they want you."

"Do you know of any openings at the moment, sir?"

"No, but I will put the word out that we have a bright DC looking for a transfer."

"Thank you, sir."

Weeks went past and Winston was starting to believe he would never get a transfer, when one day he was called into his supervisor's office.

"Well DC Sweet, you know what they say about London busses: you wait for one then three come along at once. There are two vacancies, one in Manchester the other in Bristol."

"Thank you sir, how do I proceed from here?"

"You will be asked to go for an interview at their HQs and then if they are happy with your interview you can choose."

"When will I have to go sir?"

"It won't be long, maybe a week or so. Good luck, Sweet, whichever you choose. That's all, back to your duties."

Winston finished his day's work and made his way home. He unlocked the door to his parents' flat.

"Hi Mum, I'm home. Good news."

"Hi love, what's the news?"

Winston hung his coat on the coat rail in the small hallway and walked through to the kitchen where his mum had just finished the washing up.

"Me and your dad have just finished tea, do you want anything?"

"No, I had a kebab on the way home."

"I'll make a cup of tea, go and say hello to your dad and I'll bring the tea through."

Winston walked into the sitting room. His dad was relaxing in a large green-grey armchair.

"Hi son, I heard you tell your mother you've got some news?"

"Hi Pop, yeh. I'll wait until Mum comes in and then I can tell you both. Had a good day at the market?"

"Same as usual, lifting dead animals from here to there all morning."

"Are you on earlies tomorrow?"

"Yeh, start at three-thirty so it's an early night for me tonight."

"You not going down the pub for a pint?"

"No, not tonight."

Lizzy brought the tea and placed it on the coffee table in front of Zach.

"Well love, what's the news?"

"I've been offered an interview for a DC at Manchester and at Bristol. I just need to do well at the interviews and I'm a DC."

Zach got up from the chair and shook his son's hand vigorously.

"Well done son, it's what you've always wanted since you were a boy. One more step on the road to being a chief superintendent."

"Let's not get too enthusiastic, Dad."

Lizzy was a little more restrained. She would soon be losing her son. She knew in her heart he would go sometime but now the reality was almost upon her, she wished he had a steady girlfriend and could have found a position in Brixton. But maybe he would move back later in his career.

"Well done, love. When will you know?" Lizzy sighed.

"The sarge said probably go for the interviews in a week or so, then I should find out three or four weeks later."

"Where would you rather go, Bristol or Manchester?" Zach asked.

Winston thought for a second. "Manchester I think, there will be more opportunities up there. Bristol might be a bit of a backwater."

"Well, time to celebrate. Let's go to the pub for a drink. Can't stay long, though, must be up early," Zach smiled.

Winston and his mum and dad walked to their local pub. They just had the one drink for Zach's sake but they would make a better job of the celebration on the weekend when there was no need to get up early for work. The three walked back to their flat arm in arm. Lizzy was trying to put a brave face on the news but in her heart she was not looking forward to her boy leaving home.

Winston went to bed with a mixture of pain and pleasure. He was glad he would be moving up the ladder in the police force, a bit sad to be leaving home but the big secret in his life was the fact his parents didn't know he was a homosexual. He slept an uneasy sleep that night, thoughts of how his parents would react to him being gay crept in and out of his mind. He knew that one day he would have to tell them, but not at this moment in time.

A few weeks later his interview was set up in Manchester. He headed north on the early train. He found the police headquarters quite easily and, with a few directions, was soon sitting outside the personnel officer's office where he was to be interviewed. He sat uncomfortably in the first of four dark blue plastic seats. He looked up and down the long cream-painted corridor. Police officers walked past him without acknowledging he was there. Another candidate sat down, not next to him but on the farthest blue chair from him.

"Good morning, you here for the DC's post?" Winston spoke in a cheerful voice.

"Yes, I am," the man in his twenties answered. He was smartly dressed in a blue chalk-line suit, his neatly-folded raincoat over his arm. Winston could tell from his cold voice and body language he did not want the conversation to go any further. He wondered if he should have worn a suit and not the brown cord trousers, white shirt, brown tweed tie, brown cord jacket and brown scarf he was wearing. *No, they are more interested in what I can do than what I look like,* he thought.

The door opened opposite them. Both men looked at the fat lady who just about fitted in the door frame.

"Mr Tyler?"

The man sprang to his feet, and brushed the raincoat over his arm twice with his hand as if there was something on it.

"Come this way."

The woman retreated back into the office followed by the suited man. Winston noticed he had a sticky sweet wrapper stuck to the heel of his foot. He opened his mouth to tell him but the man had gone. Winston looked down at this shoes to make sure he had nothing stuck to his own shoes. He waited. About half an hour passed then the door opened and the fat lady was there again.

"Be about another fifteen minutes. There's a canteen down the corridor and second on the left if you need a drink or the toilet, love," she uttered in a broad Mancunian accent.

"Thanks, but I'm OK."

Sure enough, fifteen minutes later, chalk line suit with sweet paper walked out. He looked down at the floor, then noticed Winston was looking at him. He tried to lengthen his neck and look up but there was disappointment in his eyes.

The fat lady opened the door.

"Mr Sweet."

Winston stood up, cleared his throat and walked after the lady into an outer office.

"Go through."

Winston knocked on the door to the interviewer's office.

"Come in." A sweet voice beckoned him.

Winston opened the door. A woman in her early forties stood up and put her hand out. Winston shook her hand. The woman was very attractive with long, flowing auburn hair which cascaded over her shoulders and onto her white silk blouse. The top two buttons of the blouse were undone and Winston could just see the lacy edge of her white bra. A few freckles powdered her slim, pointed nose. She wore bright red lipstick and had light blue-grey eyes. Winston noticed her long fingers, bright red nail varnish and no wedding ring. He thought, *If I were not gay she would be a quite intimidating interviewer.*

She went through his life, his exams, why he wanted to make his career as a detective. At the end of the interview he thought he had done well. She thanked him and told him she would write to him when she had interviewed all the applicants for the job.

***

The interview for the DC's post in Bristol was entirely different. He arrived, waited for a few moments then he was shown into Detective Chief Inspector John Orchard's office. There were two wooden desks. Orchard sat at the one in front of a large metal-framed window with venetian blinds. His desk was tidy; pen and pencils were in lines on the top of the desk, papers and folders neatly piled.

The other desk was a shambles with pens and pencils stuck in a mug with a broken handle, files everywhere. A younger man sat at this desk. He turned and nodded to Winston.

"Good morning, DC Sweet. Nice to meet you. Please sit down, and Floyd, go and get this man a tea or coffee."

"Coffee please, two sugars."

DCI Orchard was a man in his fifties, dressed in a navy blue three-piece suit, white shirt and a dark blue tie with a thin red stripe and a thinner white stripe running diagonally. He had short grey hair and a square face. Piercing blue eyes stared at Winston.

"Good trip down?"

"Yes sir, all the trains were on time."

"I've been reading your file, Sweet, you've

progressed well so far."

"Thank you, sir."

DS Floyd placed a mug of coffee in front of Sweet. Orchard leaned across the desk, picked the mug up and put a beer mat under it. He looked at Floyd and tutted.

"Now DC Sweet, this is how we work here."

Orchard went on to explain the ins and outs of how he ran the CID at Trinity Road Police Station, then he went into Winston's career. The interview went on for a long while, question were asked and answered.

"Is there anything you want to know about us, DC Sweet?" Orchard asked.

"Don't think so, sir, you have covered everything."

"OK lunch-time, my treat."

Floyd looked at Orchard.

"You can come as well, Floyd."

"Thank you, sir."

The three men walked to the police canteen. They had steak pie, mashed potato and peas, tea, and rhubarb crumble and custard.

"How do you manage to work after that lot?" Winston asked.

"This is a once-in-a-blue-moon moment, Sweet," Floyd said with a smile.

Winston caught the train back to London, hoping he would be offered the post. He got on well with Orchard and Floyd and thought he could learn a great deal from them.

All he could do now was wait for the letter.

Chapter Eight

Move to Bristol.

Two weeks and three days later the first letter arrived. He had been offered the position in Manchester. Winston had mixed emotions he was glad he had been offered the position but he wanted to work in Bristol. He decided to call DCI Orchard.

"Orchard."

"Good morning sir it's DC Sweet I came for the interview a couple of weeks ago."

"Ah Sweet I remember, have you received the letter yet?"

"No sir, I have been offered a post in Manchester but I would rather work with you but I am not sure if you offered me the position."

"Dam postal service, I sent a confirmation letter offering you the job the day after the interview."

"So I have the job?"

"Yes Sweet just write and confirm, but I will take this conversation as you are accepting the DC job at Trinity road police station."

"Thank you sir, thank you so much."

"No need to thank me Sweet you were the only candidate anyway."

Winston replaced the receiver "Yes!" he beamed as he made a fist and punched an imaginary person in the stomach.

When Winston finished his shift he walked home, his mum and dad were out so he made a cup of tea sat at the kitchen table and wrote two letters one to the Greater Manchester police declining the position of DC, the other letter to Avon and Somerset Constabulary accepting the post of DC. He placed the letters in envelopes and put his coat on ready to walk to the letter box and he wanted to get them in the post as soon as possible. He was on his way out of the door when his mum and dad came walking along the balcony.

"Hi son off out?" Zach said.

"Just off to the post box, won't be long will tell you all about it when I get back."

Winston pushed the two letters into the post box with delight, he heard the letters flutter down into the box and felt this was the beginning of a new stage in his life.

We went home and told his mum and dad that he had accepted the job in Bristol, they asked how long it would take for the transfer to go through. He wasn't sure but he would let them know as soon as he did.

The next day at work he told all the some of his friends.

"Bristol fucking dead end job that Winnie." His best friend on the force grumbled.

"Oh piss off Jim." Winston answered.

Most of the other officers congratulated him but there are always one or two who tried to bring him down with snide remarks. He tried to find out how long it would take to get the transfer through but everyone he asked had a different idea. The average seemed to be four weeks but on one really knew.

Then one day a letter arrived and told him to report to Trinity road nick in the St Paul's area of Bristol in just over two weeks time. He would have to find his own accommodation so he needed to get to Bristol a couple of days before he started work.

When he told him mum and dad Lizzy cried, Zach felt the same but kept his feelings under wraps. The guys at the station threw a big going away party and the last time he walked out of Brixton police station it was a sad affair.

His parents had organized another farewell party with friends and family at their flat that was a good night as well, Caribbean calypso's sounded late into the night, and most people went home happy and drunk.

Winston had the weekend to get down to Bristol, find somewhere to live, unpack and settle in so he could start at Trinity road first thing Monday morning.

Saturday morning arrived with a headache, Winston staggered into the kitchen, his dad was st at the table caressing a cup of tea.

"Morning son."

"Morning dad, I've got a rotten headache."

"Me too, but it was a good night wasn't it?"

"Sure was, where's mum?"

"She gone to the shop to get you some fresh cooked ham for your sandwiches."

"Is she drunk."

"What yer mum, no never, sober as a judge, the water in the kettle is hot if you want to make yourself a cup of char."

Winston took a match from the box and lit it turned the gas on the cooker ring and lit it, woosh the gas burst into a roaring blue flame. Winston shook the kettle there was not enough water to make a mug of tea. He took his favorite mug out of the cupboard and looked at it.

"You takin that son?"

"No I would rather have it here when I come home."

Zach stretched across the kitchen table and picked up The Sun newspaper. The headline HMS Sheffield hit by Exocet missile.

"Those bloody Argie's are killing our blokes out there." Zach gasped.

"Not more killed dad."

"Yeh hit one of the ships."

They both turned towards the door as they heard the key turn.

"Must be mum."

"No surly not."

"Your a sarcastic sod dad."

"Hi love, how's your head." Lizzy kissed Winston on top of his head.

"Not too bad, I have taken some paracetamol's."

"Did you get the ham and the rolls?" Zach asked.

"Sure did."

"What time is your train to Bristol love?"

"Two fifty six."

"OK plenty of time, have you packed yet?"

"Just a few more things to get in the case."

There was a tearful goodbye as Winston boarded the train to Bristol, Winston's mum and dad waved as the train slowly pulled away from the station. Zach tried to comfort his wife but she was upset as tears trickled down her cheeks.

Winston had a pleasant train ride just about one and a half hours later he was walking out of Temple Meads train station not far from the center of Bristol. He had been in contact with one of the personal officers at Trinity road and she had recommended a small bed and breakfast place near the station where he could settle down for a few weeks, find his feet and look for something more permanent. He found a taxi rank outside the train station and told the driver where he wanted to go.

"Stayin long or just here for a break?" The Asian taxi driver asked.

"I got a job here so I will be here for a while."

"Wot you doin?"

"I am a policeman."

Not another word uttered from the taxi driver. He dropped Winston off at the B&B and sped away down the street. Winston bumped his case up the three stone steps to the Park View Guest House. Winston stood outside and looked around. *No park wonder why it's called Park View.*

He rang the bell, a few moments later a woman in her fifties with hair dyed with a blue rinse and glasses that looked like butterfly wings glared at him from behind one of the glass panels in the door.

"Yes can I help you?"

"I have a room booked." Winston shouted through the panel."

"Wot? speak up."

"My name is Sweet, I have a room booked."

With some trepidation the woman unlocked the door but still kept the chain on.

"What did you say your name was?"

"Sweet, I phoned and booked a room."

The woman eyed him up and down and the pushed the door closed a little, un-hooked the chain and opened the door.

"The booking said you are a policeman."

"I am."

"But your black."

"I know I'm black." Winston reached into his jacket pocket and pulled out his warrant card and showed it to the woman, she eyed it for what seemed like a long while.

"You had better come in then, this way."

Winston pulled his suit-case into the hall.

"My name is Mrs Lewis, I run this place on my own so I have to be careful who I let in, my hubby died a few years ago, so I am on my own."

Mrs Lewis explained the rules and regulations of her guest house, breakfast times, what time he had to be in at night, if he was working late he had to phone her and make arrangements to get in, no visitors after eight at night, rules, rules, rules. Eventually she showed him to his room, on the first floor, number seven.

"My lucky number." Winston said.

Mrs Lewis either didn't hear or purposely ignored him.

The room was nice, clean and smelled of lavender, a single bed with a blue eiderdown cover, a comfortable looking arm chair, bed side table with a lamp, she explained the toilet was down the passage outside his room.

"Thanks Mrs Lewis, it looks fine."

"So I should think so."

"Any chance of getting something to eat?"

"We only serve food in the summer, you will have to go out."

Mrs Lewis gave him his key and told him to pick up a front door key on his way out. Winston sat on his bed and looked around, he felt flat, everything seemed grey and lifeless. Half an hour later he found Mrs Lewis, picked up a frond door key and walked down the steps on to the pavement. He walked for a while but still never came across a park, he found a pub open that served food and had steak pie and chips. He called his mum and told he he had arrived safe and sound. Winston wandered back to the guest house it was still quite early so the chain was not on the door.

He slept well that night. Sunday he relaxed found his way to the police station tried to acquaint himself with the area, went to the same pub and had hotpot for lunch. He watched TV in the guest house lounge, this was the only room he was allowed to smoke, he was not supposed to smoke in his room, Mrs Lewis thought her guests would fall asleep with a lighted cigarette and she would be burned alive.

He didn't sleep well Sunday night he kept thinking about the job and if he had made the right decision.

Chapter Nine.

Awkward Meeting

Detective constable Winston Sweet had worked at Trinity road police station for a few years now. He'd learned a lot from his colleagues DCI John Orchard and DS Nick Floyd. Recently they'd been working on a particularly difficult murder case. An Indian man, Mr Patel, had been murdered and his body disposed of in a bonfire on 5th November, Guy Fawkes' Night. After much forensic evidence and exhaustive investigation, there was little evidence to suggest who had killed him. L:

One line of enquiry for DC Sweet was to find out about stolen supermarket trolleys. He had to interview a young lad called Dylan Campbell and in the course of the questioning made the boy cry in front of his mum and other police officers in the room. This was completely against what Winston wanted: not for a second did he mean to upset the boy.

He finished that shift feeling depressed and sad despite knowing he was only trying to get to the truth and help with finding the killer of Mr Patel. Winston walked the streets for a long in the rain before he realized it he was standing outside The Elsinore, a pub not far from the city centre. He had visited the bar a few times before and knew it was frequented by men of his sexual persuasion.

Winston entered the bar. It was warm and he felt a little more at ease. He ordered a JD and coke, then another and then another. During the next few hours he met the next love of his life: Michael. Michael was a good-looking man in his late twenties, blond hair short at the sides and a little longer on the top, deep blue eyes, a small gold ear ring in his right ear, well-defined cheek bones and a slight tan from using a sunbed he had at home. He was the type of person that no matter what he wore he looked fabulous.

Winston spent the night with him and over the next few months the relationship developed into a love affair. They spent as much time together as they could, which was limited due to Michael working nights at the The Elsinore and Winston working all hours at the police station, trying to solve the Patel case. When they could be together they would go to the cinema or eat out.

One of their favourite places was No. 49, a smart and expensive cocktail bar in the centre of Bristol. It was owned by Leon Brown, a well-known Bristol businessman. Michael had met Leon Brown and wanted to work at No. 49 but nothing had come to fruition at the moment. What they both didn't know was that Leon Brown was the crime lord of Bristol. A black yardie gangster, he was into prostitution, drugs, guns and human trafficking. Any way Leon Brown could make money, he did. He was a suave, sophisticated black man. He wore the best clothes, ate the best food, drank the best wine. Leon was smart. He didn't have a police record, not even a parking ticket, and never got himself into any situation he could not control to the nth degree.

Over the next months the Patel case was

getting nowhere. Winston's boss DCI Orchard had hit a stone wall and after reaching retirement age had left the police force. Orchard's second-in-command, DS Nick Floyd, had passed his inspector's exam and had taken over all DCI Orchard's old cases.

This was the year DC Winston Sweet passed his detective sergeant's exam and was now DS Sweet and second to Floyd. The two had worked together for a long while and trusted each other implicitly. DI Floyd was still not aware DS Sweet was homosexual but it would not have made any difference if he had known: he had the greatest respect for his junior detective.

Winston and Michael decided to move in together and become full-time partners. Michael lived in a small bedsit in an area on the outskirts of Bristol, so they decided he would move into Winston's flat. Even though Winston only had one bedroom it was much larger than Michael's place. About a month later Michael gave notice on his bedsit and moved into Winston's flat. They were getting on so well.

One evening they had been to the cinema and had stopped on the way home for a pizza. Winston sat opposite Michael at a small table near the window. The two decided what they were going to eat: Winston was having a Diavola and Michael a Margareta, also a beer and a green salad each. The waiter came to take their order and lit the small candle which was in the middle of the table. It illuminated both their faces in a warm glow. Winston looked into Michael's eyes with love and lust. He was unaware of anything else around him. Then he was brought back down to earth with a bump.

"Winston, how are you?"

Both men looked up into the face of Nick Floyd. Hanging on to Nick's arm was his wife, Jane.

With an anxious voice Winston asked, "Sir, what are you doing here?" and stood up.

"Going to eat? Not a good detective, are you Winston?" Nick jested with a smile. Jane tugged his arm.

"Leave him alone, Nick, you've embarrassed the poor man."

"Embarrassed, no."

"Are you going to introduce me to your friend," Nick said, looking at Michael.

"This is an old school friend, Michael."

Michael stood up, looking daggers at Winston. He thrust his hand out towards Nick who shook it with vigour. Michael's hand felt like a wet lettuce to Nick.

"This is my wife, Jane. You two have met before, haven't you?" he said, looking at Winston.

"Yes we met at the last Christmas party."

Michael shook Jane's hand.

"Leave them alone, Nick, they're halfway through their pizzas," Jane suggested tugging Nick's arm again.

"Perhaps they want us to join them?"

Winston's heart sank like a stone in a pond.

"Nick, leave them." Jane forcibly pulled Nick away.

"See you tomorrow, DS Sweet."

"Yes boss."

Nick and Jane found a table at the other side of the pizza house and sat down.

"What's wrong with you tonight Nick? You

could see they wanted to be alone. You've had too much to drink."

"What do you mean, on their own? Too much to drink?"

Jane glanced across at Winston's table. Michael glanced back with a false smile on his face.

Michael returned his gaze to Winston he gritted his teeth.

"Are you ashamed of me?"

"No, why?"

"You told them we were at school together."

"I know, it was a shock seeing my boss standing there, no I am not ashamed of you."

"Sounds like you are ashamed of something then."

"Not ashamed exactly, it's just that no one knows I'm gay outside of our small circle."

"Are you ashamed of being gay then?"

"No, well no, I just haven't told everyone."

"So you are ashamed?"

"No, let's talk about this when we get home. Not here, not now."

Michael felt a welling up of tears, but he fought them back.

"OK, I'll wait until we're home. I am not hungry anymore, let's go."

"You haven't finished your pizza."

"I couldn't eat it now."

Winston asked for the bill, picked it up, looked across at Nick and Jane, lifted his eyes and walked towards the cash desk.

"They're going, and they haven't finished their meals," Nick said.

"I thought you were a good detective, love.

Can't you see they're together."

"Of course I can see they're together."

"No, I mean *together*, a couple."

"You mean they're queer?"

"That's not nice, Nick."

Nick felt his face flush with embarrassment.

"Sorry, you're right, love. So you think Sweet is gay?"

"Yes. Have you not noticed anything at work?"

"No, never gave it a thought. Bloody hell." There was a pregnant pause for a moment. "Anyway what are you eating?"

"Just a pizza and a glass of wine. I seem to have lost my appetite a bit."

"Sorry love, I've been a bit of an ass."

"Don't say anything tomorrow at work."

"No dear. I mean, yes dear."

"Promise?"

"I promise."

Winston and Michael made it home in an awkward silence. They sat up late into the night going over and over what had happened and where they were to go from here. Then, as lovers do, they made up and went to bed. They did come to one decision: at the next opportunity Winston was going to introduce Michael to his parents and was going to tell them he was gay.

The next day nothing was mentioned about the pizza house by either Nick or Winston. They got on with their work and said little. There were a few moments when looks and unspoken words passed between the two men but both tried to pretend the previous night's encounter was normal.

Chapter Ten.

A Visit To Mum

Michael decide to tell his mum first about the relationship with Winston. Michael's mum already knew he was gay: from a young age she realised he was not as other boys. She wasn't overjoyed with the situation when she first became aware, but over the years she had come to accept the fact he was homosexual. Michael's dad had died four years ago. He had never accepted his son's homosexuality but kept his feelings and disappointment to himself.

On the next day off that the two had together, they caught a bus to Lawrence Weston on the outskirts of Bristol. Michael was happy to be seeing his mum because he hadn't seen her for a month or so. They walked from the bus stop past the few local shops overlooking a small green where kids were playing on their bikes and fooling around. It was a bright day so both men were in a happy mood.

They arrived at Michael's mum's house, which was a dark grey brick two-story end-of-terrace with a small grassed front garden surrounded by a wooden fence that had seen better days.

"I must come up on my next day off and try and fix that fence up," Michael announced.

"I'll give you a hand if you want."

Michael gripped Winston's arm and said, "I love you."

Michael walked up and opened the door.

"Hello Mum, it's me."

Michaels mum appeared from the bedroom.

"You didn't tell me you were coming. Why didn't you phone?"

"Thought I would surprise you."

Michael bent a little and kissed his mum on the cheek. Doris was a short woman just about five feet tall, mid-fifties, long straggly brown hair with a lots of grey and pale blue eyes. She looked older that her years and was always cold. Winston thought she looked a bit like Grandmama from the old black and white TV series *The Addams Family*. Michael's mum was wearing a large hand-knitted cardigan, skirt and slippers. She peered around her son at Winston standing in the doorway.

"Who's he?"

"He's my partner, Winston."

"Partner? You mean you're living together."

"Yes Mum."

Doris turned and walked into the kitchen.

"Suppose you want a cuppa?"

"Yes please, Mum."

"Does he drink tea?"

"His name is Winston, Mum."

Winston followed Michael and Doris into the shabby kitchen. A black and white cat was sleeping on one of the kitchen chairs.

"Chase him off if you want to sit down."

Winston tipped the back of the chair up but the cat was having none of it. She dug her claws into the chair cushion and both cushion and cat slid onto the floor.

"Bloody cat," Michael said.

"You leave her alone, she's the only

company I have. You never come to see me these days. Living with your fancy man, you haven't got time for your poor old mum."

"I'm busy at work, Mum, please don't start."

Doris made a pot of tea in a big old brown tea pot and place it on the table in front of Winston.

"Shall I get the cups, Mum?"

"Well, if you want me to do everything."

Doris opened the fridge and took a half-filled bottle of milk out·and placed that on the table. Michael got some cups from the cupboard and blew into them before he put them on the table next to the milk.

"You saying my cups are dirty, Michael?"

"No, just a bit of dust on one."

Doris sighed and grunted.

"You going to pour?"

Michael poured the tea. Winston put two sugars in his and sipped it with a little apprehension. It was nice, very nice.

"Lovely cup of tea, Mrs Price."

Doris looked at him and grunted again. The atmosphere in the kitchen was strained and tense. The cat had pushed its way through the cat flap in the door and was now sitting on the outside window ledge looking in. Winston thought, *Even the cat is looking accusingly at me.*

"How have you been, Mum?"

"All right, but no thanks to you."

Michael looked into his mother's eyes. She looked frail and there was a frightened look.

"Can't go out at night because of all the yobs and the police are useless."

"I'm a policeman, Mrs Price," Winston

said.

"See what I mean? Useless, and they're even taking coloureds these days."

"No need for that, Mum."

"What, can't even say what I want in my own house now? I don't know what this country in coming to: yobs, blacks, foreigners. When I was young you could leave your door unlocked and everyone knew everyone."

The next thirty minutes were awful. No one spoke very much and when they did it was snide remarks and put-downs. You could cut the air with a knife.

"I think it's time we left, Winston," Michael sighed.

"Right,"

Winston drained the last few drops of tea from the cup. Doris walked into the room next door and Michael followed her.

"What's wrong with you, Mum? You know I am gay."

"Are you blind? He's a black man."

"I know and I love him. Can't you understand that?"

"No, and I don't want him here again."

"Well, if he isn't welcome you won't be seeing me."

"I don't see you now, son."

Michael felt a knife plunge into his heart. He knew he was selfish and should see his mum more often, but there was always another reason to put off the visit. Mother and son walked back into the kitchen. Winston was standing up, waiting to go.

"I will try and get some extra patrols round here at night, Mrs Price," Winston said.

Doris looked deep into his eyes. She could see he was a good man and felt a little guilty she had given him a hard time, but she was a proud woman and was not going to admit it.

They left the house Michael looked back at his mum standing in the doorway.

"I need a drink," Winston mumbled.

"Bloody right." They found a large pub called The Kings Arms on the corner of two roads and walked through the car park and into the lounge bar. Winston ordered the drinks and they decided to take their drinks outside into the beer garden. Winston placed his pint on the wooden bench table and sat down next to Michael.

"Well, that didn't work out quite as planned," Winston said.

"Sorry Winston, my mum can be a bit of a bugger sometimes."

"It's OK, but perhaps you should try and see her more often."

"You're right. I know you are right, and I will."

"Let's hope the meeting with my mum and dad goes better."

"God, I hope so."

The two men sat enjoying the last rays of a watery sun as it dipped below the large trees which lined the edge of the beer garden, and after a while, a little deflated, they made their way home.

Chapter Eleven

Winston Tells All.

The next weekend both Winston and Michael were off duty so they arranged to catch a train to Brixton so Michael could meet Winston's mum and dad. This was going to be a difficult Saturday and Sunday as Winston's parents didn't know Winston was a homosexual. He had called his mum and told her he was bringing a friend down to meet them but nothing else.

His mum said she would organise an extra bed in Winston's bedroom for the men to sleep in. They caught an early train from Temple Meads to Euston. They were both nervous as the train glided out of the station. Winston sat opposite Michael and they both stared out of the carriage window as the tapestry of houses, fields, trees and level crossings sped by. Michael went to the buffet bar and bought two coffees and a coronation chicken sandwich.

"The price of this food in bloody ridicules," Michael snapped.

Winston nodded in agreement but his thoughts were somewhere else.

Both men visited the toilet on the one and a half hour journey but it was more nerves than full bladders.

By the time they arrived in London, a light rain was falling. This seemed to match their mood and they walked down to the tube station. It was an easy route: the Victoria line straight through to Brixton. Twenty minutes later they were standing outside the station. The misty rain chilled their bones as they made the short walk to Winston's parents' house.

"There are a lot of people about, Winston, is it always like this?"

"Usually more crowded than this. This is quite quiet."

They walked along the balcony with the misty rain driving over the iron railing in a sombre mood. Winston sighed and pushed his door key into the lock.

"Here goes."

He pushed the door open and saw the beaming face of his mum. She skipped towards him and flung her arms around his neck and held him tight.

"Winston, it's so good to see you. Come in, take your coat off."

"Hi Mum, where's Dad?"

Just then Zach appeared and pulled his son close. Michael thought. *Bit of a different welcome than at my mum's.*

"This is Michael."

Lizzy grabbed Michael's hand.

"Nice to meet you, Winston hasn't told us much about you."

"Nice to meet you too, Mrs Sweet."

"Call me Lizzy, and this is my husband Zach."

"Pleased to meet you, Zach," Michael said and they shook hands.

"Come into the kitchen and we can have a cup of tea. What is this news you have to tell us?"

"I've made the put-you-up in your bedroom. Sorry Michael we don't have a big flat," Lizzy said. "Are you a policeman as well? Do you work together?"

"Mum, let him catch his breath before all the questions."

The three men sat around the kitchen table while Lizzy made the tea.

"Thought we would go out for a curry tonight, son. Do you like curry, Michael?"

"Um yes, Zach."

"So you two work together, do you?"

"No Dad, Michael works in a bar in Bristol."

"Oh, so you met in a bar?"

"Yes Dad, a gay bar."

"We have a couple of gays down the market. They're like a couple of women sometimes. One is a big guy, body builder, but as queer as a nine bob note," Zach chuckled.

Lizzy put the tea down on the table and opened a packet of chocolate digestive biscuits. She could tell Winston was not comfortable about what her husband was saying and she had a hollow feeling in the pit of her stomach.

"So what's the news, Winston?" Lizzy gushed in a demanding tone.

"Let them have their tea, love," Zach said.

"OK but I hope it's good news, don't want anything to spoil the visit."

They talked some more about how Winston's job was going and other inconsequential stuff.

Winston looked at his mum and blurted out.

"Michael and I are partners."

"What do you mean, partners?"

"We live together."

"You mean you share a flat together?" Zach said, dunking a chocolate biscuit in his tea.

"No Dad, we live together. We are partners."

There was a stunned silence. Zach with his mouth half open expecting the taste of chocolate to flood his mouth instead the tea soaked digestive biscuit dropped into his tea with a splash. He jerked back.

"Now look what you have made me do."

"Sorry Dad."

"What do you mean exactly, partners?" Lizzy questioned.

"We are partners, lovers."

"I can't believe my ears. It's your fault, you've turned him," Zach accused Michael.

Michael opened his mouth ready to say something.

"No he hasn't turned me, I have always felt this way."

"What way?" Lizzy quizzed.

"I have always like men."

"You were all right until you went to Bristol."

"No I wasn't. I had two or three boyfriends here before I moved."

"Boyfriends yes, but not lovers."

"No, lovers."

Zach stood up and put his head in his hands.

"I can't believe it, my boy a puff! Well, you are not sleeping with him under this roof, you, you..."

"You what, Dad? Queer, puff, gay boy? What Dad?"

"I don't know."

Zach's eyes were filling up. His mind was like a beehive buzzing, buzzing.

"I can't help it, Dad. I tried to deny I was gay for years but I am in love with Michael and there is nothing I can do about it."

"Love, love? You don't know the meaning of the word. All you want is sex."

"I think we had better go, Michael, this is not helping."

"No wait, let's calm down and talk about it," Lizzy said.

"Dad's not going to talk, Mum. He's as mad as hell."

Zach walked out of the room and into the bathroom. He looked at himself in the mirror. He recognized his face, although it was older than he imagined. He stared into his own eyes. It was like looking at someone he was not quite sure about. Thoughts, pictures, emotions overloaded his brain. He remembered Winston when he was born, a baby, a toddler, going to school, holidays, good, times bad times, nursing him through illnesses... thoughts, thoughts. He turned the water on. It swirled and it went down the drain hole. He splashed cold water on his face and he looked at himself again.

He is still my boy, my love, my dreams.

Zach picked the towel up and dried his face. He walked back into the kitchen and looked at Winston who was now standing and looking like he was about to leave. Michael was standing next to him, holding his hand. Zach's blood raged and boiled in his veins.

"Sit down you two, let's talk this through."

"I thought you wanted us to go?"

"Sit down."

Winston sat and Michael sat next to him. Zach sat opposite Winston, while Lizzy stood behind her husband and put her hand on his shoulders.

"Shall I make some more tea?" Lizzy said.

"I think we need something stronger than tea, love. Go get the bottle of brandy left over from Christmas."

They talked until the small hours. Winston explained about when he was a child and how he hid his feelings even from himself for a long while. Michael told Lizzy and Zach about his upbringing, about how he was abused at school by one of the teachers, how Winston was the one positive thing in his life, about his depression. There were tears and more tears that sometimes turned into uncontrollable fits of laughter. By the time it was bedtime the four people were exhausted and fatigued, worn out and drained.

"Do you want us to leave, Dad? Because if Michael leaves I go as well,"

"No son, stay here tonight. We can talk some more in the morning."

Zach and Lizzy talked sat in bed and talked quietly about their son being gay. Neither could sleep: their minds were on fire with all sorts of different scenarios.

"Do you think it was how we brought him up?" Zach whispered.

"No, it's something to do with his genes."

"So there was nothing we could have done differently?"

"No, it's just the way he has turned out."

"So I suppose there is not too much point worrying about it. We'll just have to learn to accept the fact."

"Yes but that's easier said than done."

"I read somewhere if you are in a situation

like ours, if you can't handle it you have to pretend and in time you will come to accept the situation."

"That's the plan then, PRETEND."

"Suppose so and then one day..." Zach shrugged and he felt emotion start in the pit of his stomach and rise through his body and exit through the tears running down his cheeks. Lizzy said goodnight. She turned the bedside light off and they snuggled down under the covers.

Winston and Michael had a similar in-bed chat but theirs was a little more constructive. They decided not to have too much physical contact for the visit and keep cool about what was being discussed. Winston turned the light off and they also snuggled down under the covers.

The rest of the weekend was stressful for all concerned. They talked everything through over and over again, but by the time for Winston and Michael to return to Bristol a quiet acceptance prevailed. Winston did understand how his mum and dad felt and Lizzy and Zach tried their best to understand their son. It was hard for all of them. Lizzy thought how strange it was their son had not changed and if he had come home with a girlfriend the atmosphere and dynamics would have been entirely different.

Over the next few months Lizzy came to terms with her homosexual son. Zach tried but couldn't quite accept it.

But time is a great healer and the most important thing to Zach was he didn't want to lose his son, his flesh and blood. The bond of fatherhood would overcome all.

The End

Thank you for reading my novel if you enjoyed it please can you leave an honest review good or bad.
Thank You.

<u>Free on Amazon</u>
<u>Free from Smashwords</u>
<u>Free from Barnes and Nobel</u>
<u>Free on iTunes</u>

Sign up for the author's New

Releases mailing list and get a free

copy of the second novel in the

Liston Pearce trilogy

"Consumed By Fire"

Click here to get started:

www.stephengane.com

Consumed By Fire

Book 2

In The Liston Pearce Thriller
Series

It's Bristol, the St. Paul's area, August
1990. Liston Pearce, who used to be the

gang boss, is in prison.

Leon Brown is the criminal mastermind now running every illegal money-making racket. His empire is on the up but he still wants to expand into new ventures: drugs, prostitution, protection and now people-trafficking and gun-running.

There's Mr Patel's body to dispose of too. The police hit a wall of silence and false alibis. Three members of Leon's yardie gang are becoming loose cannons.

When Liston is released from prison Leon has to make a decision. And what is he to do with those gang members who can't handle the pressure?

Printed in Great Britain
by Amazon